W9-BUD-154

Summer Days and Nights

Wong Herbert Yee

Christy Ottaviano Books
Henry Holt and Company
New York

Summer days, so warm and bright,
Paint my room in morning light.

As cat naps in a patch of sun,

My summer day has just begun!

In the meadow where daisies grow,
I creep along on tippy-toe.

Behind a clump of rocks I stoop,
Up and over, down swip-swoop!

What's this inside my net?

Hmm . . . no butterfly just yet.

Summer days can get so hot,
Makes me steam like a teapot.

Beneath an oak tree in the shade,
I sip an ice-cold lemonade!
What else is there to keep me cool?

Ker-SPLASH! I jump into the pool.

An insect whizzes past my head.
It zips into the flower bed.
Buzz-buzz-buzz!
What's this I see?

A black-and-yellow bumblebee!

Summer's eve, before it's dark . . .
HOORAY! A picnic in the park.

From tree to tree,

I run and hide. . . .

WHEE! I shoot straight down the slide.

We spread a blanket on the ground,
Plates and napkins passed around.

Guess who comes to join the fun?

Black ants marching one by one!

A golden sun sinks in the sky,
Another summer day gone by.

Summer nights, too hot to sleep,
From the windowsill I peep.
I hear a noise . . .
a scritch-scratch sound.
Something's creeping on the ground.

Who is there outside my house?

Why, it's just a tiny mouse!

A shadow drifts across the grass.
I duck and wait as it floats past.

Hoo-hoo, it cries. . . . Who's calling me?

Oh, look! A barn owl in the tree.

Summer nights, moonlit skies,
Winking, blinking fireflies.

I hear a splash, see something jump.
A voice croaks low: *ba-rump, ba-rump!*

A summer breeze blows through the trees.
It bends the branches, rustles leaves.

Across the field, on past the gate . . .

My eyelids droop, it's getting late.

I crawl in bed,

Turn off the light . . .

And dream of summer days . . . and nights.

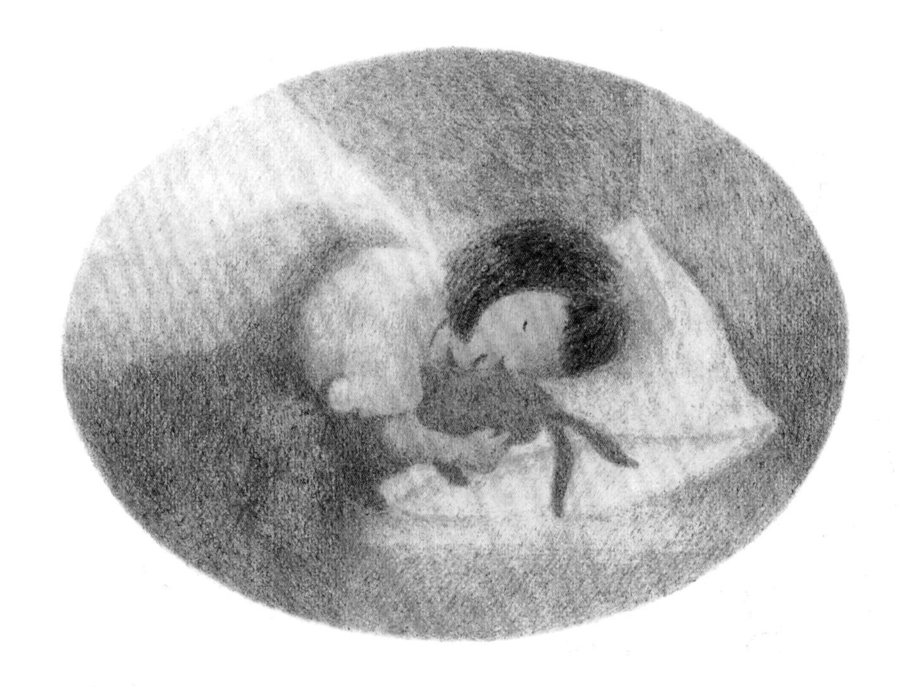

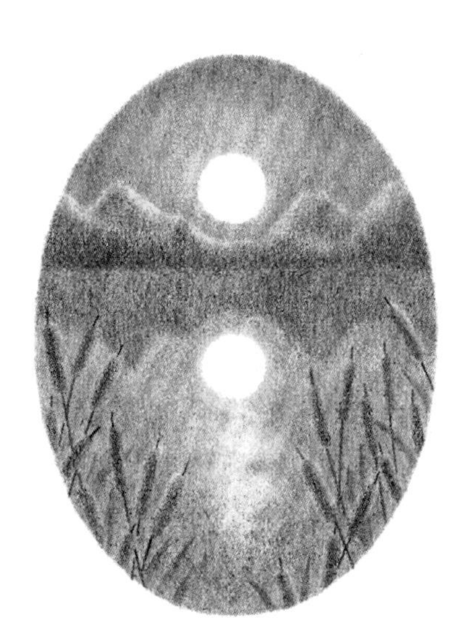

For Lily, Ella, Cameron, Corbin, and Lily Joy

Henry Holt and Company, LLC
Publishers since 1866
175 Fifth Avenue
New York, New York 10010
mackids.com

Library of Congress Cataloging-in-Publication Data
Yee, Wong Herbert.
Summer days and nights / by Wong Herbert Yee — 1st ed.
p. cm.
"Christy Ottaviano Books."
Summary: A little girl enjoys the activities of a a warm summer day and night.
ISBN 978-0-8050-9078-9 (hc)
[1. Stories in rhyme. 2. Summer—Fiction. 3. Day—Fiction. 4. Night—Fiction.] I. Title.
PZ8.3.Y42Su 2012 [E]—dc23 2011028598

First Edition—2012 / Designed by Véronique Lefèvre Sweet
The artist used Prismacolors on Arches watercolor paper to create the illustrations for this book.
Printed in China by South China Printing Company Ltd., Dongguan City, Guangdong Province.

10 9 8 7 6 5 4 3 2